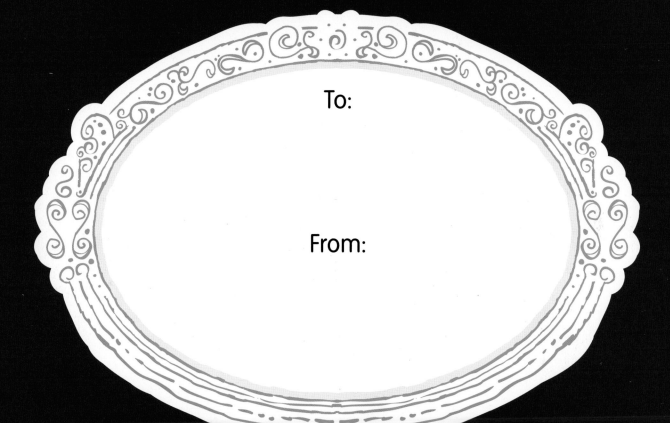

To:

From:

# HOME FOR THE HOLIDAYS

A Little Book about the Different Holidays That Bring Us Together

words by Craig Manning
pictures by Ernie Kwiat

SESAME STREET

sourcebooks
wonderland

We all have traditions we celebrate each year
with family and friends that fill you with cheer.

With such joy in your home, your heart starts to soar.
There are so many things to be grateful for.

It's about time with family and those you love most,
in a place you belong, where you're always held close.
It's the things that you do and the laughter you share
when being together with people who care.

It's a feeling of lightness and brightness and good
that shines through your heart and your whole neighborhood!
It's knowing that kindness and hope are the spark
to bring joy to the world and light up the dark.

It's about being grateful for all that we share,
for all our family and friends, no matter where.
This time of the year, we know that it's true:
we're thankful for all of the love that shines through.

And what about gifts? They're part of it too!
But not just the presents given to you.
It's giving to others or doing nice things,
and the smiles that your love and company brings.

The holiday season's about playing together,
and having good fun, no matter the weather!
It's taking the time to make memories that last,
though the days spent with friends may go by too fast!

It's being with loved ones, from near and from far,
who send their best wishes wherever they are!
You can still keep in touch with those far away
and remember the people who aren't here today.

It's what's in your heart: being merry and bright,
and the way that you share it each day and each night.
It's the spirit of joy, and knowing it's real
just from the way all the holidays feel.

It's music and sound, played quiet or loud
on drums or guitars or sung with a crowd.
The traditions bring us together, we know,
and we'll only find new ones to add as we grow!

As the year ends, celebrate all that we've done,
but when a new one begins, there'll be even more fun!
So many tomorrows and new things to do.
Where will you go? You know it's all up to you!

It's a time to be kind to whoever you meet:
to those in your town or those down the street.
To family and neighbors and friends you have found,
spread your good wishes to those all around.

And if there's one big thing the holidays teach,
if there's one single lesson we want you to reach,
it's letting LOVE guide you wherever you go,
and the peace you can feel from letting it show.

Our holidays may differ in meaning and name,
but the things that we cherish are often the same.

There's a truth we all know, wherever we roam:
at this time of year, there's no place like home!

# Home for the Holidays

**NOTE FOR GROWN-UPS:** People around the world celebrate their heritage with a diverse range of cultural holidays. The following includes more detailed information about the wonderful holidays featured in this book to explore further with your child.

## Eid al-Fitr

Eid al-Fitr (*the festival of breaking fast*) is observed to mark the completion of the holy month of Ramadan and the end of fasting. Eid al-Fitr is characterized by a sense of renewal, joy, and celebration. Many Muslims start the day by praying at their local mosque, community center, or home, followed by visits with loved ones to celebrate and enjoy special holiday meals. The day can involve varied and unique traditions depending on where you're from.

## Diwali

Diwali, also known as "Divali," "Dipawali," or just "the Festival of Lights," is India's biggest holiday but is celebrated all over the world and in the United States. It takes place in October or November each year. The holiday gets its name from a row (or "avali") of clay lights (or "deepa") that people light outside their homes during the holiday. The lamps symbolize the holiday's purpose: to celebrate the triumph of light over darkness, or of good over evil. Diwali celebrations include decorating, sand art, games, feasts, gift exchanges with friends and family, fireworks, and sky lanterns.

# Thanksgiving

In the United States, Thanksgiving is celebrated on the fourth Thursday of every November. Typical celebrations include a big harvest feast, gatherings of family and friends, and reflections on the things people are thankful for. It's a great way to share gratitude! Many other countries have similar holidays to Thanksgiving around harvest time, such as Canada, China, Germany, Japan, and more.

# Hanukkah

Hanukkah is a Jewish Festival of Lights that takes place over eight days. Celebrations include lighting the menorah (a candleholder with nine candles), exchanging gifts, and eating a variety of traditional foods from potato pancakes to jelly doughnuts. During Hanukkah, children also play with the dreidel, a four-sided top with Hebrew letters on each side.

# Kwanzaa

Kwanzaa is a Pan-African and African-American holiday that celebrates African heritage, culture, and tradition. Each year, Kwanzaa lasts seven days, from December 26th to January 1st and includes family and community celebrations with gift-giving, music, and feasts. One key symbol of the holiday is a candleholder called a Kinara that holds seven candles. Each candle stands for one of the seven principles of Kwanzaa, which include unity, self-determination, responsibility, community cooperation, purpose, creativity, and faith.

# Christmas

Christmas is a Christian holiday. Holiday traditions vary around the world, but often include family gatherings, big feasts, decorations of colored lights or Christmas trees, and gift exchanges. In the United States, children hope for the arrival of Santa Claus in a sleigh led by reindeer, to deliver presents under the tree. Other cultures have their own Santa Clauses, such as "Father Christmas" in Great Britain, "Sinterklaas" in the Netherlands, and "Père Noël" in France!

# New Year's

New Year's is usually celebrated over two days each year: December 31st and January 1st. The holiday marks the end of one year and the beginning of the next according to the Gregorian calendar, which much of the world follows. Around the world, people stay up until midnight to mark the arrival of the New Year with fireworks, confetti, and festivities! One popular tradition is the making of "New Year's Resolutions," goals that people wish to pursue in the New Year.

# Chinese New Year

Chinese New Year celebrates the beginning of a new year according to the Chinese calendar, or lunar calendar, which varies depending on movements and phases of the moon. Chinese New Year starts on the last day of the last month following the lunar calendar, called Chuxi. The first day of the coming New Year (also following lunar calendar) is Lunar New Year's Day, called Chuyi. The public holiday lasts for seven days and is called Spring Festival. Chinese New Year revolves around traditions and customs aimed at attracting good luck, wishes, and fortune for the year to come. Festivities include feasts, fireworks, and even parades through the streets with a long figure of a dragon.

Cover and internal design © 2021 by Sourcebooks
Cover and internal illustrations © Sesame Workshop
Text by Craig Manning
Illustrations by Ernie Kwiat

Sourcebooks and the colophon are registered trademarks of Sourcebooks.
Published by Sourcebooks Wonderland, an imprint of Sourcebooks Kids
P.O. Box 4410, Naperville, Illinois 60567–4410
(630) 961-3900
sourcebookskids.com

Source of Production: Wing King Tong Paper Products Co. Ltd., Shenzhen, Guangdong Province, China
Date of Production: June 2021
Run Number: 5021982

Printed and bound in China.
WKT 10 9 8 7 6 5 4 3 2 1